Huxley Pig's Aeroplane

Rodney Peppé

WARNE

For Toby Floyer

Other books about Huxley Pig
Here Comes Huxley Pig
Huxley Pig the Clown
Huxley Pig's Dressing-up Book

FREDERICK WARNE

Published by the Penguin Group
27 Wrights Lane, London W8 5TZ, England
Viking Penguin Inc., 40 West 23rd Street, New York, New York 10010, USA
Penguin Books Australia Ltd, Ringwood, Victoria, Australia
Penguin Books Canada Ltd, 2801 John Street, Markham, Ontario, Canada L3R 1B4
Penguin Books (NZ) Ltd, 182-190 Wairau Road, Auckland 10, New Zealand

Penguin Books Ltd, Registered Offices: Harmondsworth, Middlesex, England

First published 1989
10 9 8 7 6 5 4 3 2 1

Copyright © Rodney Peppé 1989

ISBN 0 7232 3623 2

Printed in Hong Kong by
Imago Publishers Ltd.

Early one morning, Huxley Pig was woken by the sound of the door-bell. A parcel had been delivered.

His Granny had sent him a wonderful present. "An aeroplane!" said Huxley. "Just what I wanted!"

Huxley got dressed and played with his plane. He zoomed on his bed...

He zoomed
on his table...

and he zoomed
on his chair.

When Huxley had finished zooming he found a letter, hidden in the wrapping-paper. His Granny was coming to visit him.

"I'd better tidy up," thought Huxley, "or she'll think I live in a pigsty!"

"It might be easier, though," he said, "if I could go to see her in my plane…"

He rolled to the left . . .

and he rolled to the right.

And then the engine began to cough. "Perhaps," thought Huxley, "I had better land."

It was rather a bumpy landing.
"Terrible pilot!" said
Horace, the mechanic.

"The plane's
making funny
noises,"
said Huxley.
"No problem,"
said Horace.
"I'll fix it!"

So Horace worked on the plane,
while Huxley had lunch.

"Is that it?" asked Huxley, when he thought Horace had finished. "I'll take her up for a test flight, to make sure," said Horace. "Hop in the back."

Huxley felt a raindrop. Then another... and another. "It's going to rain," he said.

"Rubbish," said Horace. "Look at the sun."

And they flew through a rainbow. "I've never done that before," said Huxley. "Oh, I do it all the time," said Horace.

Then it began to grow dark. "Thunder," said Huxley. "We're in for a storm." "Storm ... what storm?" said Horace.

And they flew into a storm. "I can't see where we are," cried Huxley. "Please pass me the map."

"Catch," called Horace, tossing the map over his shoulder.

Oh crumbs!

"That wasn't very clever," said Huxley. "Now I can't find my Granny's house!"

You'll have to find it without me!"
said Horace, buckling on his parachute.
"I don't like storms!" And he jumped.

The plane zoomed up and
Huxley nearly fell out.

He tried to scramble into the pilot's seat,
but the plane was out of control.

Wheeee! The plane plunged through the clouds into the tree-tops to... CRASH!

Huxley woke up with the sound still ringing in his ears! "Have I been dreaming?" he wondered. "But I've got Horace's spanner ... and his hat! Impossible!" thought Huxley as he realized, "It's Granny at the door!"

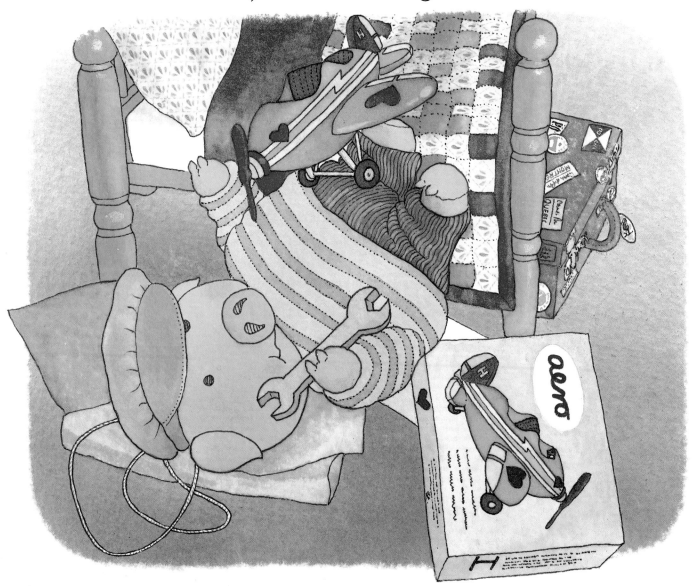